**What was Indiana Jones doing
in New York City in spring 1914?**

Indiana Jones is that world-famous, whip-cracking hero you know from the movies....

But was he *always* cool and fearless in the face of danger? Did he *always* get mixed up in hair-raising, heart-stopping adventures?

Yes!

Read all about Indy as a kid...watch him come to the rescue of a fiery labor organizer who is marked for death...and get ready for some edge-of-your-seat excitement!

Young Indiana Jones books

YOUNG INDIANA JONES™

and the

CURSE OF THE RUBY CROSS

By William McCay

Random House 🏠 New York

Copyright © 1991 by Lucasfilm Ltd. (LFL)
All rights reserved under International and Pan-American Copyright Conventions. Published in the United States by Random House, Inc., New York, and simultaneously in Canada by Random House of Canada Limited, Toronto.

Young Indy novels are conceived and produced by Random House, Inc., in conjunction with Lucasfilm Ltd.

Library of Congress Cataloging-in-Publication Data
McCay, William.
    Young Indiana Jones and the curse of the ruby cross / William McCay.
        p. cm.
    Summary: While visiting New York City in 1914, teenaged Indy runs across his old friend Lizzie Ravenall and becomes involved in retrieving a stolen family heirloom for an immigrant Italian labor organizer.
        ISBN 0-679-81181-8 (pbk.)—ISBN 0-679-91181-2 (lib. bdg.)
        [1. Adventure and adventurers—Fiction.]   I. Title.
    PZ7.M4784136Yo   1991
    [Fic]—dc20   90-53242

Manufactured in the United States of America
    2   3   4   5   6   7   8   9   10

YOUNG INDIANA JONES™

and the

CURSE OF THE RUBY CROSS

Chapter 1

Whistling a cheery ragtime tune, Young Indiana Jones stepped out of the theater. New York City's Union Square hustled and bustled around him. Indy stood and took in the scene.

The streets were full of horse-drawn wagons and cabs. And autos! Indy had never seen so many autos in one place. On the sidewalks were people rich and poor—from young "swells" in fancy suits to immigrant workmen in baggy trousers and cloth caps.

Indy tipped his fedora hat back on his head. He felt very big-city, coming out of a matinée. The show had been great! Jugglers and comedians and magicians. Chorus girls who sang and danced—in tights! There was nothing like this back home in Utah.

Oh, Indy knew it wasn't the best New York had to offer. This was 1914, and the big stars had left Union Square for the new theaters near Forty-second Street. But Indy wasn't complaining. He'd seen his first New York show. So what if he'd had to go on the sly?

That morning his aunt Mary had sent him out once again "to improve his mind." She'd been ruining Indy's spring vacation ever since he and his father had arrived in town. Indy's aunt used to teach school. So while Professor Jones did research at local universities, Aunt Mary filled up Indy's time—"usefully." She had a bee in her bonnet about Indy "not getting an education."

That was the way Aunt Mary saw it. Indy had had some amazing adventures traveling with his globetrotting dad. But he was a little short on book learning.

"You put in less than half a year at that English boarding school," Aunt Mary complained. "And even then you were off on harum-scarum adventures instead of studying. You're fourteen years old, young man, and you know nothing. Absolutely nothing!

You'll never get into a college at this rate."

So instead of enjoying the spring weather, Indy was stuck making field trips and writing reports. And then Aunt Mary *graded* them.

Professor Jones wasn't getting a vacation either. But that was his choice. He was busy writing a paper on the Normans—thousand-year-old dead guys who didn't interest Indy a whole lot. Maybe because his father talked about them all the time.

Today Professor Jones had gone off to New Haven to visit the Yale University library. Indy was supposed to spend the day at the Metropolitan Museum of Art, up at Eighty-second Street and Fifth Avenue. "The *whole* day," Aunt Mary had instructed him. "There's a great deal to see."

The morning was okay. Indy had liked the exhibits of knights' armor and weapons. And he'd stared longingly at the ancient relics from Egypt and Greece that archaeologists had dug up. He knew that someday *he'd* be doing that kind of work.

But the art galleries? Indy decided to skip them. What did an archaeologist need to know about a bunch of old pictures? Indy wanted to taste some big-city life.

"I can make up something about the paintings for Aunt Mary," he told himself. "You see one picture, you've seen them all. It's not like mummies, after all."

After lunch he'd walked from the Eighties down to Union Square at Fourteenth Street. The nickel carfare he saved paid half the price of a cheap seat in the theater. Now, after the show, Indy jingled his pocket money and soaked up the excitement of Union Square.

It wasn't a square, really, just a large open space in the middle of the city. Three big streets came together here. The air was full of traffic noises—car horns, shouting drivers, and most of all the bells of trolley cars. Several sets of trolley tracks ran through the square. Subways rumbled underground. Along the west side of the square stretched a park, its newly leafed trees green-gold in the late afternoon sun. Beyond the park rose tall office buildings—ten stories, at least.

Indy watched a trolley clatter by. Should he jump aboard and take the easy way back to Aunt Mary's apartment? His feet, tired after a three-mile walk, voted to ride.

But before Indy could move, he heard

voices in the distance. The sound of chanting grew louder and louder. Finally he could make out the words. "Votes! Votes! Votes for women!"

The noise was coming from the south, from Broadway. Indy ran along Fourteenth Street to the nearest corner. He saw an open car chugging up Broadway with a grim-faced woman standing in the rear. Behind her stretched a huge parade of hundreds of women. A group in caps and gowns marched under a large banner that read LAWYERS. After them came doctors, teachers, and other professions. A crowd of young women strode briskly by—bookkeepers and stenographers.

Indy stared, fascinated. He'd read about women fighting for the suffrage, the right to vote. But they hadn't seemed quite real. Now, right in front of him, live suffragettes were tying up New York City's streets!

People gathered on the sidewalk to watch as the parade marched into Union Square. Some cheered and waved. But a lot of the men—and some women, too—made fun of the marchers. A few policemen appeared, trying to keep the rapidly growing crowd off the street. But it was too hard.

An elbow jostled Indy to one side as two roughnecks pushed past him. "Hey, Pinkie, pipe these dames," one of the men said. He scratched his face under a two-day growth of whiskers. "They wanna vote? Do they think us men are gonna be sucker enough to let them?"

The pink-faced man beside him let out a belch that made Indy's head swim with beer fumes. "Say, some of them are kinda cute. Howzabout that blond one over there?"

Indy glanced where Pinkie was pointing—and froze in disbelief. He knew that girl! Those glowing blond ringlets under the perky straw bonnet—those bright blue eyes—that pretty face . . . it was Lizzie Ravenall!

He could hardly forget Lizzie. A year ago they'd almost gotten killed together searching down south for her family's lost fortune. All through that adventure, Indy's heart thumped like mad whenever Lizzie came near. He'd been sad when they'd parted in Washington. But what was Lizzie doing here in New York? And how did she get into this parade? She and a petite brown-haired girl were waving a yellow banner that read VOTES FOR WOMEN—*NOW!*

12

The two slobs pushed out of the crowd and into the street. "Hey, blondie, forget about this voting nonsense," Pinkie yelled at Lizzie. "Let us men do the thinking."

"Right!" Whiskers tore Lizzie's end of the banner out of her grasp. Her brown-haired partner found herself in a losing game of tug-of-war.

"Stop it!" the girl cried.

"Make me," Whiskers said, sneering. More nasty-looking characters broke through the police line, joining the fun. They jostled and heckled the marching women.

Lizzie leaped to her friend's help. But Pinkie pushed her back hard.

"Leave her alone!" yelled Indy. He cannoned through the crowd, his hands bunched into fists. He was ready to paste the big lug.

But someone beat him to the punch.

A brawny, dark-haired young man charged from the other side of the street. His handsome face was flushed with anger. The stranger grabbed Pinkie by the arm, whipped him around, and slugged him. The big drunk fell, out cold.

And with that, all of Union Square erupted in fights. Indy was caught in a riot!

Chapter 2

People shoved Indy every which way. Newcomers jumped into the fight. Others tried to flee.

Over the roar of the riot, Indy heard shrill tweeting sounds. Police whistles! Reinforcements had arrived.

Police wagons rolled up, and men in blue jumped off. They waded into the crowd and began cracking heads with their nightsticks. Anyone fighting—male or female—got hit. But Indy noticed that only the suffragettes—the marchers—were dragged off to the wagons.

I've got to get Lizzie out of here, Indy thought. He clawed his way between fighters to reach her. She was trying to pull free from Whiskers. The big heckler was using her as a shield while he punched at the dark-haired fellow who'd come to the rescue.

Indy jumped into action, kicking at Whiskers' leg. Lizzie got loose, the man half turned, and the young dark-haired guy socked him squarely on the chin. Whiskers wobbled for a second, a silly look on his face. Then he joined his pal Pinkie in dreamland, dropping to the pavement like a chopped tree.

The young man grinned at Indy. "Thank you, friend." His voice had a slight accent.

Lizzie caught hold of Indy's arm, goggling. "Indiana Jones!" she exclaimed. "What are *you* doing here?"

"I was just about to ask you the same thing." Indy staggered as the crowd suddenly pushed back and forth. He was almost separated from Lizzie and her newfound friend.

"More coppers!" a voice yelled. "Run if you don't want to get thumped—Yow!" A man sped by, clutching his head. Blood trickled between his fingers.

A club-swinging police officer headed for

the young woman who'd marched with Lizzie. She threw the banner they'd been carrying over the cop's head.

For a second she grinned triumphantly at Indy, Lizzie, and the young man with them. Then a blue-clad arm shot out of the crowd and caught her by the shoulder. "I saw that, missy," an angry policeman growled.

The young man stormed forward.

"No! Get away!" Lizzie's partner yelled as two policemen hauled her toward a paddy wagon. "Don't worry! My brother will—"

Indy couldn't hear any more. The crowd surged, nearly knocking him off his feet. If he fell, he'd be crushed by running people. Lizzie tightened her clutch on his arm, and grabbed onto the young man's. "Minna's family will get her out. But what about us?" Her face was pale.

"Come on!" Indy tugged his companions forward. They had to get away from the bottom of the square, where the police were. But as they headed north, they saw another line of cops forming up there.

"More bluebellies!" Lizzie wailed, getting really scared. "Where can we—"

"This way," their new friend cried. He

pulled them west through the crowd, toward the park.

A horrible cry rose as the mob crashed into the second line of police. The cops moved forward steadily, their clubs rising and falling as if they were beating a gigantic drum. Rioters retreated back down the square, shoving against those behind them. Now the tightly packed people were trapped.

Tripping over trolley tracks, dodging elbows and knees, Indy's little group fought their way through the crowd. Indy could hardly breathe.

Finally up ahead they saw the iron gates of Union Square Park. Only a small knot of hecklers blocked their way.

"Hold it, sister," one of the toughs said, reaching for Lizzie. "Yer wearing yaller flowers, like all dem suffrage gals."

Indy glanced at the corsage of yellow daisies pinned to Lizzie's dress—a dead giveaway. Lizzie whipped up her umbrella to knock the thug's hand away. The handle caught the man in the head. It hardly seemed to touch him, but the guy dropped. His friends backed off.

"That's Dr. Latson's method of Women's

Self-Defense," Lizzie said smugly as they dashed through the gates.

"That doesn't explain why that guy fell," Indy said. He hefted Lizzie's umbrella and looked shocked. "Someone put lead in this handle. It's weighted to hit harder!"

"That's a trick I learned from the girls in the clothing unions. It's very handy on picket lines." Then it was Lizzie's turn to look shocked as their new friend tore the umbrella from her grasp.

"The cops catch you with this, they'll lock you up." The young man tossed the umbrella into some bushes. "And get rid of those flowers!"

Lizzie wordlessly obeyed the man's orders.

Indy could hardly believe what he was seeing. The Lizzie he knew never did anything without an argument. But here she was, doing just what this stranger told her. To make it worse, she did it with hero-worship in her eyes.

They ran across the lawns of the park with dozens of other frightened people. The trees hid the disaster going on behind them in the square.

The young man slowed as they left the park on the far side. Bright blue eyes twinkled in his olive-skinned face. Indy was surprised. The man looked Italian—yet he had a Viking's eyes. He grinned, flashing white, even teeth at Lizzie. "No more of those—what did you call them? 'Bluebellies'?"

Lizzie blushed. "I forget I'm in a Yankee city nowadays," she said. "That's what folks back home in North Carolina used to call the Northern soldiers—because of their blue uniforms." She smiled shyly. "I'm Lizzie Ravenall, by the way. And this is my friend Indy."

"Roberto Normanni." The young man took Lizzie's hand and bowed. He had a strong chin and a chiseled nose—he was a very handsome guy.

Indy liked this less and less. "If we hang around here holding hands, the cops are gonna catch us."

Even as he spoke, groups of people came boiling out of the park. Right behind them came the tweet of police whistles.

"You're right, Indy," Roberto said with his slight accent. He quickly started them down one of the side streets that led away from the square. "Indy," the young man repeated, a questioning look in his eyes. "That's an odd name."

"It's a nickname," Indy explained shortly. "From Indiana. I'm Indiana Jones."

"Glad to meet you, Indy."

They continued along the street for several blocks. The uproar behind them died away. Lizzie breathed a deep sigh.

"So where have you been, Indy?" she asked, turning to him. "I wrote to you, but the letters kept coming back. You kept moving, I guess."

Indy turned pink with pleasure. Lizzie had tried to write to him! Too bad he never got the letters.

Then Indy went red as he realized he hadn't ever written to Lizzie. "Well, I, uh, was all over. Egypt, Russia, England . . . you know how Dad is always off to places." He gave her a short account of what he'd been up to.

Both Lizzie and Roberto looked impressed.

"So, uh, how has life been treating you?" Indy asked. "When I left Washington, you were going to start classes at Georgetown University."

Now it was Lizzie's turn to be a little embarrassed. "Things didn't turn out as we expected," she said. "I had a big shock after you left. It wasn't so easy to claim the treasure my grandfather had hidden—"

Indy looked surprised. "I thought all you had to do was get some court papers and you'd have your inheritance."

Lizzie's jaw set. "Not exactly. Because I'm a girl—"

And how! Indy thought.

"The judge thought I needed a guardian! Me!" Lizzie still fumed at the idea. "Just because my folks are dead! I can take care of myself. I went to school and worked for my own money. I helped find the treasure! But that judge treated me like—like a *child!*"

"Who did they choose for your guardian?" Indy asked. Knowing Lizzie's headstrong ways, he had a lot of sympathy for whoever got the job.

"At least it was a friend," Lizzie admitted. "Dr. Walton."

Indy rolled his eyes. Poor Dr. Walton! He

was a famous teacher of history who knew all about the days of the Civil War. But the elderly man couldn't always deal with life today—and could never handle Lizzie. So Indy wasn't exactly surprised at what he heard next.

"I started taking classes at Georgetown," Lizzie began. "And I found some other women who felt the same way I did—angry at the way we're treated. Then I met a group called the Congressional Union—women fighting to get the vote. And I decided to help them."

Roberto Normanni smiled. "Like you helped today?"

Lizzie smiled back. "I went on a few marches. But I never got arrested," she said. She sounded almost disappointed. "Then Dr. Walton found out and decided I should leave Washington. He got me accepted at Barnard College, the women's college of Columbia University." She shook her head, grinning. "He never guessed there might be suffragettes in New York, too."

Lizzie glanced back the way they'd come, toward Union Square and the riot still raging. "This was my first march up here. It's a lot bigger than anything I'd been on before." She bit her lip. "A lot more violent, too. All I've done up here so far is organizing."

"That's what I do," Roberto Normanni said. "Organize."

He looked from Indy to Lizzie. "Back home in Sicily, I cut the stone to build the churches. Here I help build the big buildings. It's not an easy job, my friends. Long hours of dangerous work for pennies. Bosses who do not care about our safety. Thousands of us die working. Hundreds of thousands are hurt, even crippled. And the big-money men brag that they doubled their profits."

The young Italian's face was angry. "There's only one way for a simple workingman to stand up to the rich—by organizing. In union there is strength. So I organize for the union."

Lizzie looked impressed. "Union organizing—isn't that pretty dangerous?"

Roberto shrugged. "Sometimes." He pointed to a scar that disappeared into his heavy black eyebrows. "I got that from a management goon about a year ago."

Great, Indy thought, watching Lizzie's eyes

widen. Now she thinks he's an even bigger hero. She was hanging on Roberto's every word. But luckily Roberto didn't seem to notice.

Another set of police whistles twittered. "It's not safe for you to stay with me," Roberto told Lizzie. "We could still get arrested. Cops don't like union organizers—or their friends."

Roberto rushed them along, heading farther west. "I think the Ninth Avenue elevated train will get you back to Columbia. Here we are." They stood at a stairway that led up to the El station.

"But I don't want—" Lizzie began. She looked at her watch. "Is that really the time?"

For a second she looked sweet and confused. Indy's heart swelled in his chest. Then Lizzie had to spoil it all by looking adoringly at Roberto. She'd never looked at Indy that way.

"I hope I'll see you again," she said to Roberto a little shyly. "Good luck—and stay safe."

She started up the stairs, then remembered Indy was there. "How about you, Indy? Do you have to go home?"

Indy shook his head. "I've already missed supper. And I'm in no hurry to see my aunt. She'll probably skin me alive."

"I can't help with your aunt," Roberto said with a grin. "But I can help with supper. Why not come home and eat with my family?"

"Uh—great. Thanks!" In spite of his jealousy, Indy found himself liking the young immigrant.

"Well, good-bye, fellas," Lizzie called from the stairs. "You can get in touch with me through the Barnard dorms."

Indy gave Lizzie his aunt's name and address. "We're on the telephone, too."

As he gave her the number, they could hear a train approaching. Lizzie darted up the rest of the stairs. "Have a nice time," she called back.

Indy sighed. He'd have a nicer time with Lizzie there. But Roberto didn't think she'd be safe. Was the Italian really such dangerous company?

Chapter 3

"Where do you live?" Indy asked Roberto as they started off.

"In Greenwich Village, south of Washington Square," Roberto replied. "Thompson Street. A whole lot of immigrants from Italy live there. I stay with my aunt and uncle and a couple of their friends."

"Friends?"

"Well, lodgers," Roberto admitted. "New York apartments cost money. Five dollars a week for a four-room apartment. It's good to have extra people to help pay."

They headed south. A few blocks later Indy wondered if he'd walked into another country. Crowds and pushcarts filled the crooked streets. People bargained loudly and chatted with one another in fast-paced Italian. Every once in a while he heard a word that sounded familiar from his Latin lessons. Even more rarely he heard a word in English.

Spicy smells of a hundred meals cooking in a hundred apartments filled the air. The buildings in the neighborhood were made of cheap red brick that had quickly turned dingy. The five-story apartment houses were crammed together without even an alley in between. Indy realized that unless you had a room at the front or rear of the house, you wouldn't have a window. He mentioned that to Roberto, who nodded.

"They do have air shafts," he said, looking grim. "But there's no light in them, and the air stinks of garbage."

Roberto stopped in front of a building that seemed a little cleaner than the others. "This is it," he said. "We have to walk up to the fifth floor." He grinned at Indy and joked, "If you're not hungry when you begin, you'll be hungry at the top!"

The apartment door opened right into the kitchen. Roberto's uncle, Signor Catania, was a heavyset man who didn't speak much

English. His aunt was a cheerful woman joking in rapid-fire Italian. Delicious smells came from the pot she was stirring.

As soon as Roberto and Indy came through the door, she shooed them toward the table. Three other young men joined them for plates of spaghetti. One was Roberto's cousin Silvio. Silvio and his friends didn't speak English as well as Roberto did. But they were eager to practice on a friendly American.

Indy found himself in a spirited conversation that went all over the place. He told about some of the adventures he'd had. The boys talked about their family homes in Sicily, the large island at the southern tip of Italy. Then they described how they'd sailed to America.

"We come over in steerage, the bottom of the boat," one of the lodgers said. "Too nasty even to keep the animals there." He made a face.

"Worse than animals they treat us," said the other lodger. "When we get to America, they keep us on Ellis Island in a pen. Deciding if they let us stay or not."

"We think America is made of gold," Silvio said. He glanced down at his fingernails, too grimy ever to get clean. "But it's made of dirt, just like anyplace else."

"And Silvio should know," Roberto joked. "He's always down in the dirt, digging tunnels for the subway. Or is that a gold mine you work for?"

They laughed. "It was a hard life back home, remember," Roberto said. "No one in Sicily will ever get rich with a tiny family farm. Here the work is hard, but we have hope."

His face shone. "We can build our lives. Everyone can—not just people from Italy. Poles, Jewish people, Russians, Greeks, people from China and Japan. More than a million people a year come to be Americans."

"Lots more riders for the subway," Silvio said. "New people for you to fight for too, Roberto." Silvio was obviously very proud of his cousin's union battles. "Any more trouble on the job?" He smacked a fist into his hand. "Just let me and the boys know."

Roberto spoke of the struggles of the working folk. Next came a long talk about baseball. Could the upstart Brooklyn Dodgers beat the New York Giants?

Then the mantel clock struck ten o'clock.

"How did it get so late?" Indy exclaimed. "I've got to get back to Aunt Mary's!"

Roberto put a hand on Indy's elbow, keeping him at the table. "Indy, I know you can handle yourself. But the streets at night around here . . . what can I say? There are a lot of guys who look for trouble. Didn't you say your aunt is on the telephone? Torini downstairs is too. Let's give your aunt a call. Maybe you can sleep here tonight, okay?"

Aunt Mary was happy to hear from her vanished nephew—for about ten seconds. Then it was, "Henry Jones! Where are you? What are you doing out at this time of night?"

Indy winced. His real name was Henry, but he hated it when people called him that. "You see, Aunt Mary, I met a friend of Dad's and mine. Then I had dinner with a friend of hers, and it got so late . . ."

Well, it was the truth—sort of. "Anyway, they asked me to spend the night. Here, why don't you talk to Mr. Normanni?"

Roberto was absolutely charming on the phone. When he handed the earpiece back to Indy, it was a very different Aunt Mary on the other end.

"All right, you're allowed to stay. But I want you home bright and early tomorrow. You've got a report to write. And I don't want you putting those nice people out."

Indy promised to be a good boy, hung up the phone, and followed Roberto back upstairs.

The Catania apartment was small, and sleeping arrangements were crowded. Indy wound up sharing a trundle bed with Roberto in the parlor. Silvio slept in the room, too. For a while his snores kept Indy up.

He was just drifting off to sleep when Roberto quietly got up from the bed. Indy blinked awake at the movement. He watched Roberto head to a window and drop to one knee, reaching along the baseboard. There was a muffled noise. Then Indy caught the glint of metal in Roberto's hand, a rich, yellowish gleam.

Indy squinted, a little embarrassed to be spying on his host. Roberto held the object in his hand up to the window. It was a cross!

Each arm of the cross was a good four inches long. Roberto handled the cross as if it weighed a lot. For a second it shone in the moonlight. Gold, Indy thought drowsily. Nah.

It's fake. He's a poor working stiff. What would he be doing with a real gold cross?

Indy's eyelids were heavy. They fluttered closed. He never felt Roberto return to bed.

But Indy did reawaken later in the night. He was having a terrible dream about suffocating in the dark.

Indy opened his eyes—to almost perfect blackness. The moon had set, and the room was pitch dark. This wasn't his bed! Where was he? Then Indy remembered. He was staying with Roberto Normanni. Indy shifted uncomfortably. The room was very warm, and he still couldn't breathe right.

He coughed. That was smoke!

Staggering to his feet, Indy made his way out to the kitchen. The smell of smoke grew stronger and stronger. Indy yanked open the apartment door.

The dingy stairwell was lit with a rosy glow. And as he looked down to the ground floor, Indy saw why. Five stories below, the wooden stairs were covered with rapidly spreading flames.

Indy stared in horror. The only way down was completely on fire!

Chapter 4

Indy whipped back into the apartment, slamming the door behind him. "Wake up, everybody! The house is on fire!"

The sleeping family quickly roused. Silvio bolted to the door, but Indy pulled him back.

"The stairs are on fire. We can't get out that way!"

Roberto ran to a window. "We'll have to use the fire escape." He threw up the window sash and tried to get his aunt onto the cast-iron balcony outside. Mrs. Catania clung to his arm, crying in Italian.

"Silvio, come help your mama. We have to warn the other people in the building!"

Indy joined the young men, running from

apartment to apartment on each floor. They banged on doors, yelling "Fire! *Fuoco!*"

Soon parades of frightened people were coming down the fire escapes. Silvio, now on the sidewalk, was breaking windows on the ground-floor apartment. *"Fuoco!"* he shouted, alerting the people inside.

Indy was the last in line on the front fire escape. The nearer they got to the ground, the hotter and smokier the air became.

On the second-floor balcony, Indy helped an elderly man onto the sliding ladder that led down to safety. A crowd had gathered on the street to watch the excitement. Indy stared down at the circle of upturned faces. Something was wrong . . .

"Where's Roberto?" he called to the people on the sidewalk.

Silvio yelled back, "He went to warn the people on the second floor."

Indy glanced at the windows of the second-floor apartment and realized they were closed. No one had come out of there!

He tried to peer inside but couldn't see anything. He shrugged out of his jacket, wrapped it around his hand, and smashed a windowpane. Oily black smoke poured out.

Fumbling open the window, he yelled to Silvio, "I need help up here!"

As Silvio came clattering up, Indy took a deep breath of clean air. Then he plunged into the smoky darkness. The oily cloud burned his eyes. He stumbled around, tripping over furniture he couldn't see. No, that wasn't furniture—that was a body!

"Indy!" Silvio yelled in the window.

"Over here—somebody's out cold!" Indy and Silvio carried a woman out.

"The people in the rear apartment say that Roberto warned them," Silvio said. "They got out the back. There should be three more people in here. And where is Roberto?"

Indy wondered the same thing. He headed back into the smoke with Silvio and some others. Here was another unconscious form near the window—a little boy. These people had been warned. The smoke must have knocked them out before they reached safety.

Searching blindly through the thick, choking cloud, Indy blundered onto two more people—a little girl and a man. "Over here!" he coughed. Now the rescuers had found everyone who lived in the apartment. But Roberto was still missing.

Choking and gasping, Silvio and the others gave up. The front room was like an oven. The flames must be just beyond the apartment door, Indy thought. He took a deep breath. Somebody had to check the kitchen out. It looked like he was elected.

Crawling along the floor, Indy found some smoke-free air. But the floorboards were almost scorching to the touch.

Now I know how a hamburger feels on a griddle, thought Indy. Can't stay here much longer. This whole place is about to go up in flames!

Then the apartment door went ablaze. And in the flickering light Indy saw Roberto. He was lying face-down close to the fire.

Indy scuttled across the floor, racing the flames. The scorching boards burned his palms. But he managed to reach one of Roberto's outstretched arms. Grabbing hold, he hauled his unconscious friend toward the front room. Roberto seemed to weigh a ton.

Sweat poured from Indy's body in the horrible heat. Smoke drew streams of tears from his eyes and tore at his throat. He hacked and wheezed, not even able to call Silvio for help.

They reached the front window—but the fire escape was empty. Indy realized why as he fell onto it. The metal was as hot as a branding iron. Below, he saw a flame flash out of the ground-floor window. It ran over the ladder to safety like a blowtorch.

"We can't go down," he told Roberto. His friend lay half-out the window, gulping fresh air. He was coming around. Roberto struggled all the way out, then got to his feet, leaning heavily on Indy. He looked around in confusion. "How—?" he began.

"Roberto! Indy!" Silvio's voice reached them. They turned to see Roberto's cousin on the fire escape next door. He shoved a plank across the empty space to make a bridge. "Get over here! It's the only way out!"

Indy and Roberto tottered to the plank bridge. Behind them, a huge tongue of flame burst from the window. Boy, Indy thought, we got out of there just in time!

Indy helped Roberto onto the board. The Italian crawled slowly, so slowly. Indy smelled burning leather. His shoes were smoking on the hot metal!

Roberto was across. Now it was Indy's turn. "Come on!" People were shouting encouragement. But all he could hear was the roar of the flames. Then he was in reach of the other fire escape. Half a dozen eager hands grabbed him and hauled him to safety. Indy gratefully sucked clear, smokeless air into his aching lungs.

Roberto grabbed Indy. "I can't . . . believe . . . we made it out," he choked. "You saved my life! There was a reason why . . . we met today . . . Indiana Jones."

"Sure," said Indy, a little embarrassed. "I was destined to save you . . . you haven't annoyed your bosses enough yet!"

But Silvio's face was very serious as he helped the two of them down the ladder to safety. "It's nothing to laugh about. When I got my mama down the stairs, I found something bad in the street."

They were on the sidewalk now. Indy saw a fire engine pull up. Firemen began unrolling hoses. And off in one corner a policeman was talking to the two young lodgers. They stood guard over two big tin cans in the gutter. Even from a distance Indy could read the letters on the cans. "Kerosene," he said.

"Kerosene," Silvio said grimly. "This fire was set on purpose. I think to get Roberto!"

Chapter 5

In the morning Indy got odd looks as he rode the trolley up to West Twenty-seventh Street, where his aunt Mary lived. Although he had washed, his clothes still reeked of smoke. But when he arrived at Aunt Mary's, he had much worse to face than the stares of strangers.

Professor Henry Jones was back from his research at Yale. Indy found himself standing on the carpet in the slightly cramped parlor. His father and aunt sat at the desk by the window.

Aunt Mary was tall and thin. She looked like a cartoon of a schoolmarm. But she sounded like a trained lawyer when she started her cross-examination. She quickly discovered that Indy had disobeyed orders the day before.

"So," she said tartly after she heard Indy's stumbling explanation. "You just decided to skip the art in the art museum. If you were one of my students, that would be enough to fail you. In your case, though, the punishment will be to go again—and to write a full report for me."

Aunt Mary's long, thin face was all frowns as she folded her arms. "And where did you go instead, young man?"

When she found out that he'd been in Union Square, the questions veered to the suffrage march. "Did you see the awful street fight I read about in the newspapers?" Aunt Mary asked.

Indy's dad looked at him and shook his head. "Street fights? Suffragettes? I expect you to take better care of yourself, son." Professor Jones sounded peeved. Indy knew why. His father hated to have his work interrupted. A puzzled look crossed the professor's face. "Suffragettes?" he said again. "Don't women vote already?"

"Maybe they do in Utah, but not in most

of the country." Hands on her hips, Aunt Mary confronted the professor. From her tone of voice she sounded a bit like a suffragette herself. "Perhaps a dozen states allow women to vote—in local elections. But in this great democracy half the population can't vote to elect our president. Men deny the vote to criminals, lunatics, and idiots. Could you explain why they deny it to women?"

Professor Jones actually looked embarrassed. "To tell you the truth, Mary, I hadn't really thought about it."

"Yes, it's typical of you, Henry. If it didn't happen during a crusade, you know nothing about it."

Aunt Mary was even less happy when she heard about the disaster at Roberto's house. "A fire?" Her mouth became a tight line. "I regretted letting you stay out, right after that phone call last night. You should have been safely home."

Indy looked down at the carpet. "If I'd been safely home," he mumbled, "I wouldn't have saved my friend."

Of course, he knew he was in for a stern scolding. He was a little surprised, though, that his father was the one to try it.

"This is most annoying, Junior," Professor Jones began. "I am not pleased at all. While I allow you a certain amount of freedom—"

Aunt Mary snorted. "You hardly pay any attention to the boy."

Which was worse? Indy wondered. Dad paying no attention or Aunt Mary paying too much?

The professor acted as if he hadn't heard. "I expect you to act responsibly, Junior, and not to upset your aunt. Just follow her course of study—and stop interrupting my research." The professor's eyes went to a pile of books on the desk—new studies he'd collected at Yale. "I wish to hear no more of this." He picked up a book. The lecture—and his son—were dismissed from his mind.

Aunt Mary gestured Indy out of the room. As the door closed behind him, he heard his father say, "But what's the problem, Mary? I said everything you wanted me to."

Indy was making himself a sandwich when the telephone in the hall began to ring. Aunt Mary appeared in the kitchen door, an odd expression on her face. "It's for you," she told Indy. "A girl named Lizzie Ravenall."

"Indy!" Lizzie's voice crackled over the

telephone wires. "How was your evening with Roberto?"

Of course, Indy realized, she wants to know more about Roberto. He told the story of the fire, bringing a gasp from Lizzie.

"It was set deliberately?" she said. "I bet it was to get Roberto." Indy could hear the hero-worship in her voice. "He surely was right. Union organizing is really dangerous."

It can even be dangerous for *all* your friends, Indy thought sourly. But all he said was, "How about you, Lizzie? Any problems after the march?"

"I'm a little worried about Minna Frobisher," Lizzie admitted.

"Who?"

"Minna," Lizzie said. "The dark-haired girl who marched with me yesterday. We were supposed to go to the library today, and she hasn't shown up."

"Have you checked at her dorm?"

"She doesn't stay at the school. She lives here in the city," Lizzie said. "I was thinking of stopping by her house. I don't suppose—um, ah—you'd like to go with me?" She sounded nervous.

Indy stared at the phone. Was Lizzie "I

can do anything a guy can do" Ravenall asking for someone to hold her hand?

"Meet me in front of the Plaza Hotel around noon?" Lizzie asked. "I'll explain it all then."

Indy felt out of place standing in front of the gleaming white walls of the Plaza Hotel. This was a ritzy part of town. The hotels here were twice as tall as the buildings on Union Square. The Plaza rose across from one corner of Central Park, at Fifth Avenue. A constant stream of traffic ran up and down the avenue—horse-drawn cabs and carriages, lots of new autos. A shining Rolls-Royce was parked in front of the hotel. A gray-uniformed chauffeur stood polishing the hood.

The sidewalks were filled, too—with fashionable strollers. Ladies in flowing silk and lace dresses walked delicately by on gentlemen's arms. Some of the ladies wore hats as wide as umbrellas, with enough plumes on them to feather an entire bird. The men wore elegant dark suits. Some even had tall silk hats.

Indy was wearing a skimmer straw hat instead of his usual fedora. The straw hat felt like a cheese box on his head, but it had been a present from Lizzie last year. He was glad Aunt Mary hadn't caught him in his new suit. Indy had asked his father if he could go out. As he'd hoped, Professor Jones just grunted his okay without even looking up from his book.

"I declare, Indy, you look more handsome every time I meet you!" A young woman came bursting out of a cab.

For a second Indy didn't recognize Lizzie. She was wearing an elegant violet suit with a wide, flowing skirt that stopped three inches above the ankle. It showed off her gray suede high-button shoes. Her hat looked like some sort of turban with a tall feather and a veil. "Lizzie?" he said in surprise. "I—I guess I could say the same for you. Gosh, you look pretty." He was glad he'd dressed up for this meeting.

Lizzie and Indy set off along Fifth Avenue. "Look at those women in hobble skirts," scoffed Lizzie. "That tight hem at the ankles hardly lets them walk. How can they let themselves be slaves to some Paris designer?"

"Well, girls can be pretty silly—" Indy shut

his mouth in horror, but the words were already out.

Lizzie turned on him, shaking her finger. "See? That's the way men always think of us. As girls. As slaves. That's why we've got to change things—"

"You mean—by winning the vote?" Indy said. "I never thought of it that way." He remembered his aunt's words—criminals, lunatics, and idiots. Which was the reason women couldn't vote?

They continued up the avenue. On one side of the street stretched the greenery of Central Park. On the other side were block after block of mansions. "You put on your best duds when you go calling in this neighborhood," Lizzie told Indy. "This is where all the millionaires live."

"Minna Frobisher is a millionaire?" Indy stopped in his tracks.

"Well, the Frobishers have been making money ever since the war."

Indy didn't have to ask which war. For Lizzie and most people from the South, it meant the Civil War.

"Grandpa Frobisher made a pot of money selling supplies to the Yankee army—and cheating the army officers. Minna's pa made pots more buying and selling stocks after the war. Then he went and took Mrs. F. on a boat ride to celebrate. Turned out to be the *Titanic*."

Which hit an iceberg and sank back in 1912, Indy recalled. "Were the Frobishers saved?"

Lizzie shook her head. "All the money went to Minna's big brother, Wilfred. And his big brag is that he's doubled it since the *Titanic* sank."

"So Wilfred's the millionaire?"

"He's a snob and a social climber." Lizzie made a face. "He's afraid that Minna's being a suffragette will make him look bad." She tapped Indy on the elbow. "Well, here we are."

They were standing across the street from a mansion that took up half the block. The building was of carved pink stone. A gray stone wall surrounded it, blocking the view from the sidewalk. The wall also forced passersby to keep in their place—out of the garden.

"It's—big." Indy stared at four stories of turrets, spires, stained glass, and statues.

"Ugly is more like it," Lizzie said as they crossed the street. "It's just bits and pieces of famous—and prettier—houses. Lots of money went into this pile, but no taste."

Lizzie led the way through the open gate, right up to the front door. She pulled the bell knob. A minute later a gloomy-looking butler appeared.

"Lizzie Ravenall to see Miss Minna Frobisher," Lizzie said firmly.

The butler managed to look more gloomy. "Just a moment, miss." He vanished into the shadowy hall of the big house.

"That's all right, Marchbanks. I'll take care of them." Another man came down the hall, expensive clothes slightly strained by his plump body. His round, jowly face was bright red under carefully oiled black hair.

"Miss Ravenall, I don't think we've met. I'm Wilfred Frobisher." The man crossed his arms instead of shaking hands.

"A pleasure to meet you, sir. I'm here to see Minna—"

"You're not," Wilfred Frobisher told her flatly. "Not after you got my sister arrested with this crazy voting business." He hooked his thumbs in the pockets of his vest. "It's just lucky one of the officers at the station house happens to be a friend."

"Happens to be in your pocket, you mean," Lizzie cut in.

Frobisher gave her a nasty glare, but continued. "And I was able to arrange for her freedom without any embarrassing publicity."

"Well, I'm surely glad for you, but I'd rather discuss this with Minna." Lizzie moved to pass through the doorway, but Wilfred Frobisher blocked her way.

"Minna is my baby sister, and since our parents died, I'm her guardian. That means I have to protect her."

"Protect her?" Lizzie's face went bright red. "Protect her from what?"

"From radical people with crackpot ideas who will ruin her life," Frobisher said. "People like you, Miss Ravenall, and that awful Italian—Normanni, isn't it?—who's trying to turn my own workers against me."

His face looked as if he'd detected a bad smell. "Dirty foreigners! They want to overthrow our whole way of life. You'd think somebody would weed out all the dangerous agitators at Ellis Island."

"Since when is asking for a decent living wage trying to overthrow this country?" Lizzie demanded furiously.

Wilfred Frobisher cut her off. "I wouldn't waste any pity on that Italian, Miss Ravenall." He smiled nastily. Indy hated the sight of the man's gloating, piggy eyes.

"I'd worry more for myself," Frobisher went on. "My family has donated generously to Columbia University over the years. The deans there will try their best to do anything I ask."

His cruel smile got wider.

"And I've already asked to have you expelled from Barnard College!"

Chapter 6

Oh, brother, a regular record, Indy thought later that afternoon. Two lectures in one day! At least this time he wasn't on the receiving end. Indy was sitting beside Lizzie Ravenall in the dean's office at Barnard College. Dean Sayers had spent quite some time criticizing what she called Lizzie's "out-of-school activities."

Now it was Professor Jones's turn to plead Lizzie's case.

He was doing a pretty good job of going to bat for Lizzie. Indy had begged his dad for help. Right now Professor Jones was Lizzie's only hope of staying in Barnard.

Professor Jones was very annoyed to hear

that the dean had been asked to expel Lizzie. Coming to her rescue meant losing even more time on his research. But he'd been charmed by Lizzie when he met her a year ago in Washington. And Lizzie had been sent to Barnard by his friend Dr. Walton, who was now her guardian. So he had to step in.

"Dr. Zachary Walton is a solid man in his field, Dean Sayers, and he would be most—"

Dean Sayers cut him off with a gesture. Then she reread part of Wilfred Frobisher's letter. "Dr. Walton is a respected historian, Professor. On that we agree. But my concern is more with, ah, current events."

She glanced sharply over her spectacles. "If *you* will agree to take the part of her absent guardian and exercise an authority which, I fear, the college has not been able to exert—"

"*Me?*" the professor said, horrified.

The dean nodded. "As a parent yourself, I'm sure you understand how to restrain an . . . *overeager* spirit."

Indy fought to hold in his laughter. Restrain spirits? His father usually had his nose in an ancient manuscript and didn't even know that Indy was around!

Of course, Professor Jones wasn't about to tell the dean that. "I understand, Dean Sayers. If this is the only way to keep Lizzie in the school—"

At the same time he gave Lizzie an angry "see what you got me into" look.

"I shall also need some assurances from you, Miss Ravenall." The dean switched her gaze to Lizzie. "You must understand that you will be on college probation. Any further misconduct will have to be punished. And in this case I would include any contact with radical groups—with the suffragettes or with labor agitators like Mr. Normanni— under the category of misconduct."

"I see." Lizzie looked down at the beautiful Persian carpet on the floor. "Well, ma'am, I certainly want to stay at this wonderful institution of learning. If that's what I have to do, then that's what I have to do."

Lizzie's face was a picture of meekness. *Too* meek, Indy suddenly realized. Was that the face of the girl who'd bopped a thug at the park gates yesterday? He couldn't believe that Lizzie would give in so tamely.

As soon as the dean declared the meeting over, Lizzie was on her feet. Professor Jones lingered, his eyes on the dean's bookshelves.

"I see you have the entire collection of the *Rerum Italicarum Scriptores*," he said. "Does that include Geoffrey of Malaterra's *Historia Sicula*? I'm doing some research into the Norman kingdoms, you see—"

"Not only that, I have a rare printed copy of Amatus of Monte Cassino's *Ystoire de li Normant*," Dean Sayers replied proudly.

"Professor Jones, we'll leave you to your discussion," Lizzie said sweetly. "Indy can see me back to my dorm."

"Ah. Yes." Indy's father hardly looked up.

As soon as they were out of the dean's office, Lizzie gave Indy a crafty grin. "I know a great place we can visit," she said. "Minna told me about it. It's something you see a lot of these days—a construction site."

"Any one in particular?" Indy asked, wary.

"Downtown, not far from the Plaza Hotel." Lizzie tried hard to look innocent. "It's soon to become the Hotel Frobisher."

"Frobisher? Like in Wilfred Frobisher? Minna's brother is building it?" Indy thought for a second. "Oh, no. Let me guess. That's where Roberto Normanni must be working. Didn't I hear you promise not to see him?"

"I don't want to *see* him. I've got to *talk* to him." Lizzie waved her hand as if she were dismissing something. "Besides, a promise doesn't count if you're forced into it."

Indy sighed. But he followed Lizzie as she left the campus. Soon they were paying their nickel fares and getting onto the subway. Lizzie was now his father's responsibility, but his father wasn't around. Somebody had to keep an eye on her. It was up to Indy.

A ride and a short walk later, Indy and Lizzie were back on Fifth Avenue. In the upper Fifties the area was still mainly mansions. One corner, however, was surrounded by a wooden fence. A whole parade of wagons loaded with shining white stone was drawn up by the gate.

"Look at all that rock," Indy said. "Frobisher must be spending a fortune on it."

"And on the architect." Lizzie stared up at the half-finished structure. It already rose taller than the Plaza's 19 stories. And it seemed ready to keep on going. "I think Wilfred Frobisher wants to build the first skyscraper hotel."

She frowned at the line of workmen coming out to unload the wagons. "Too bad he's being so stingy with the people who have to do the work."

The men hauling the heavy stone all looked somehow alike, strong but stringy, busy yet . . . tired. The only well-fed face seemed to belong to the foreman. He directed the construction workers in a loud voice.

"All right, you loafers, let's get all this new stone squared away. I want it all on the top floor before we leave, so we can start setting it tomorrow morning."

The man's pink face actually turned red as he heard the low groan from his men. "Well, come on, you men! The sooner it's done, the sooner you can go home."

"It's six o'clock. We're supposed to be going home *now.*"

Indy and Lizzie both turned at the sound of a familiar voice. Roberto Normanni stepped from behind one of the wagons, balancing a stone block on either shoulder. Indy heard Lizzie sigh. He could understand why. Roberto looked like a statue of Hercules come to life. He walked over to the foreman, seeming to ignore the weight he carried.

"Or are we getting overtime pay for the extra work, Mr. Dowd?" Roberto asked.

Dowd, the foreman, was not a small guy. But Roberto stood nearly half a head taller, staring down at him.

The foreman's face went an even deeper shade of red. "You guys will get whatever *I* say should be in your pay packets!"

Roberto continued to give him a level look. "We deserve extra pay for extra work."

A low murmur of agreement came from the other workmen.

Dowd was now so red in the face that Indy feared he would burst. The foreman drew back a fist. He looked ready to swing at Roberto.

But Roberto, his arms still around the stone blocks on his shoulders, didn't move. "It's not such a big deal to hit a man who can't defend himself," he said quietly. "But if you punch me, I might drop one of these stones. It might smash you."

Dowd's face went from red to pale, and his arm came down. "All right," he finally growled. "An hour's extra pay for an hour's extra work." He looked sourly at Roberto. "But Normanni, you don't leave till the job's finished. That's why you'll be on the gang hoisting the stone up."

Roberto shrugged—an impressive feat with a big stone block on each shoulder. Then he headed back through the gate.

High above the fence Indy noticed a heavy wooden beam. It jutted out from the top floor of the unfinished building, beside a pile of stone. A huge pulley hung from the beam, with a thick steel cable running over it and hanging down. Indy couldn't see the bottom of the cable. He guessed one end was attached to a steam winch on the ground.

His guess was proved right a moment later. Roberto must have started the machine up. With a screeching roar, the cable began moving. As the winch pulled one side down, the other side rose. The bottom of the rising end was split into four smaller cables, which stretched down to the four corners of an open platform.

Indy and Lizzie watched the crude elevator appear over the fence. A gang of men clung to the cables, riding the platform to the top of the building. Indy and Lizzie couldn't see Roberto inside the fence. The other workmen were out and busy, though. They passed stones from man to man until they disappeared through the gate.

Whatever happened beyond the fence was invisible to the visitors on the sidewalk. But the men worked fast. Roberto kept the winch roaring. The emptied platform came down, then rose again. This time it was piled high with stone blocks. Indy watched the platform rise steadily.

Then Lizzie gasped. Indy darted his eyes to where she was staring.

On the top floor he caught a flicker of movement. It was a figure moving away from a pile of masonry—a *collapsing* pile. The stone blocks had been stacked in a rough pyramid, and now one corner was giving way. Rocks slid off the pile, bounced off the floor, then plunged into space. The blocks fell almost lazily—until they crashed into the upward-bound platform.

It shook with the impact, the steel cables twanging like a plucked guitar string. Then the cable at one corner broke loose. The platform tipped, dumping its stone cargo.

Indy gasped. It was like a landslide, an avalanche of stone dropping onto the steam winch—and onto Roberto Normanni!

Chapter 7

Even as the mass of stone came plunging to the ground, Indy and Lizzie dashed forward. They tried to get in the gate to the construction site. But a crowd of laborers came running the opposite way.

The building stones struck with an earth-shaking crash. Then came a dull *boom!* The boiler on the steam winch had exploded.

"He's dead!" Lizzie screamed, pushing through the gate. "Roberto's been killed!"

Indy saw the tears in Lizzie's eyes. "Maybe he got out of the way," he said. But he couldn't keep the doubt out of his voice.

Inside the wooden fence all was chaos. A cloud of dirt and dust had erupted when the stones smashed into the earth. Escaping steam from the destroyed winch boiler added to the murk.

Then out of the haze stepped a bedraggled figure. It was covered with whitish dust, and its shirt was half torn off. For a second Indy wondered if it was a ghost. Then he realized it was Roberto Normanni. From the expression on his face, it was an angry Roberto Normanni. Wherever his skin wasn't coated with dust it was red with rage.

Roberto didn't even notice Lizzie and Indy. He was out the gate, yelling, "Dowd! Where are you?"

The foreman was outside the fence, shouting at the workers. "Get some buckets! We've got to put out any fires!"

When Roberto spotted Dowd, he charged straight for him. His hands clamped around the man's throat. "So you decide to smash *me*, eh? Make Mr. Frobisher happy by getting rid of me?"

"Roberto!" Indy yelled. "Let go! You're going to kill him!" He tried to pull one of Roberto's arms away—and couldn't even move it. Indy turned to the other workmen, who stood staring. "Come on! Stop him!"

It took three men to break Roberto's grip. They were just in time. The foreman was beginning to turn a pale blue from the strangling.

"Roberto, listen to me," Indy shouted into the angry young man's ear. "Dowd couldn't have set you up. How did he know you would fight with him about the overtime? You just happened to be on the hoisting winch—"

"And somebody dropped that load of stone on me," Roberto finished for him. "I was lucky to see it coming. At least I got the rest of the gang out of the way."

Now Roberto was thinking again, not just reacting to the attempt on his life. "Okay, maybe Dowd didn't try to kill me. But someone did. The guy can't burn me up, so he tries to flatten me." Roberto's face was grim. "I think Wilfred Frobisher has finally had enough of me."

"You think Wilfred Frobisher had last night's fire set?" Lizzie asked.

"Who else?" Roberto followed Dowd back through the gate. Indy and Lizzie trailed after him into the construction site. The cloud of dust had settled. They could see the wrecked hoisting platform. The steam winch that pulled it was flattened. Most of the fallen stone blocks were cracked or broken.

"No more hoisting today," said Roberto. "But we'll have to clean things up here."

The workers quickly cleared away the wreckage and then headed home.

"That was a close call," said Lizzie. She was still shaken by the attack on Roberto. "Aren't you worried?"

Roberto gave her an "it comes with the job" grin. Then he said, "Work's over. I think that's it for attacks today."

"Where are you going to stay now that your apartment house is burned?" asked Indy.

"We have lots of friends in the neighborhood," said Roberto. "Whoever has room is putting one of us up."

"Did you lose everything—furniture, your clothes, all your belongings?" asked Lizzie.

Roberto shrugged. "We came here from Sicily with hardly anything. All I need is a place to sleep. Even the floor will do." He frowned. "But there is one thing at home I must get."

"What's that?" Lizzie asked.

Roberto hesitated a moment, looking from Lizzie to Indy. Then he seemed to make up his mind.

"Come. I'll show you. I need some advice. Maybe you can help me."

He took them down to Greenwich Village. The streets were as full of people as the day before. Everywhere they saw kids playing street games.

But one part of Thompson Street looked very different. The building where Roberto had lived was blackened with smoke. Indy stared at the fire escape he had clambered along the night before. The metal frame was twisted from the heat of the flames.

Indy nodded at the sagging iron. "I sure wouldn't trust that again!"

Lizzie looked doubtfully into the burned-out doorway. The stairs inside were a total loss. Most of them were charred, and a few had disappeared entirely.

"How can you get upstairs?" Lizzie looked at Roberto as if he'd have all the answers.

And wouldn't you know it, Roberto *did* have an answer. "From the roof next door."

Roberto led the way into the neighboring

apartment house. They climbed the stairs to the roof, then crossed over to Roberto's building. Roberto helped Lizzie from one roof to the other. She looked thrilled to swing from his strong arms. Indy wished he could swing her that way.

The inside stairs hadn't burned at the top. The trip down to Roberto's floor was quick. Moments later they were stepping through the door of Roberto's now-empty home.

Everything was covered in soot. The smell of smoke hung heavy in the air. Although the apartment door was scorched, nothing inside had been burned.

"I don't know what will wash off and what will clean up," Lizzie said. "But at least you'll have some things left."

Roberto just shrugged. "There's nothing much in here. Except this."

He went to a parlor window and knelt down. Indy realized this was the same spot Roberto had headed for last night. Roberto slid his hand carefully along the wooden molding by the floor. He pressed in, and a section of wood flipped back. Reaching inside, Roberto lifted out the cross Indy had seen in the moonlight.

"This is *Il Croce Ruggiero*. It's been in my family for—well, almost forever." He held up the cross. It was about eight inches from edge to edge. The side arms seemed made of gold and were thinner than the top and bottom. That section was made of iron with gold wire wound around it. The workmanship seemed pretty crude. But there was a big red gem, almost as big as the last joint of Indy's thumb, in the center of the cross.

At first Indy thought the gem was glass, but he'd never seen glass glow like that. It had to be a ruby. That made the cross incredibly valuable. And if Indy knew anything about archaeology, the heirloom was something important. He could *feel* it, just looking at that strange old cross.

"The ruby cross has been passed from father to son for hundreds and hundreds of years," Roberto explained. "But I—I am the last of the Normannis. So when I came to America, the cross came too."

"Weren't you afraid it would get stolen?" Lizzie asked.

Roberto shook his head. "No one found it— I hid it in my luggage. The cross comes apart. See?" He pressed a barely noticeable stud just below the ruby. The whole top arm of the cross came off.

Indy looked at it closely. "I wonder why it was made like that."

"I guess the cross was made to be hidden. That's what we Normannis have done for years," Roberto explained. "When I came to live here, the first thing I did was build that secret compartment into the wall. My father beat it into my head that the ruby cross must be kept safe." He gave Indy and Lizzie a lopsided smile. "He said his father did the same to him. And on and on, back through every generation of my family."

Clicking the cross back together, he looked at his companions. "Not even my uncle and Silvio know about the cross. You are the first outsiders ever to see it. But I need your help. You know America better than I do. Where is a safe place for me to keep it?" He shook his head. "I don't know what would happen if I lost it."

"Well, yer about ta find out," a hoarse, crude voice suddenly said behind them. "If you set such store by that there cross, there's one man who'd just love to have it—just fer spite."

Chapter 8

Indy, Lizzie, and Roberto whirled from their places by the window. Standing in the parlor doorway was a big hulking man. His face was bloated and pasty white. A nasty smile displayed a jagged row of tobacco-stained teeth.

Behind him were two other muscle-bound brutes.

"How—how did you get up here?" Lizzie's voice quivered with surprise as she stared at the thugs.

"Same way you did, girlie—across the roof and down the stairs," Dough-face told her. "Surprised ya, didn't we?"

"You were following us?" Indy said.

Roberto tightened his hold on the cross. "More important, what do you want with us?"

"We just want you, Roberto Normanni," Dough-face said. "We had business with you at the work site—but we missed you."

"Missed him?" Indy repeated. "Or missed him with all those rocks?"

Beside him, Lizzie gasped.

"You got it right, kid." Dough-face and his friends crowded into the parlor. "Now we'll finish it up."

As the three plug-uglies advanced on them, Roberto slipped the cross into the waistband of his trousers and bunched his fists. Indy moved to stand beside his friend. Lizzie headed off to one side, crouching next to one of the rumpled beds.

The thugs paid no attention to her. They came at Roberto and Indy, confident in their numbers and size. That was a mistake. As they passed her, Lizzie whipped the blanket off the bed and tossed it over them.

Together, Indy and Roberto charged. They crashed into the thrashing bundle of wool, knocking the men inside over.

Indy laughed, sitting on the blanket,

thumping anything underneath that moved. "The bigger they come—" he began.

"The harder they fall!" Dough-face clawed out from the cocoon. He swung a round-house right that sent Indy to the floor. For a second Indy lay there, seeing stars. Then another thug tackled him.

This guy looked like a hairless gorilla, with a flat face and a broken nose. He and Indy rolled around like a pair of little kids wrestling and scrapping. The bad guy had the upper hand—and a strong grip on Indy's hair.

Indy was helpless until Lizzie jumped into the fight. She gave his opponent a kick in the ribs that made him jump. Indy used the chance to wriggle free.

Roberto had one of the other thugs down and was swinging desperately at Dough-face. A moment later Dough-face was holding Roberto's arms while the other thug worked him over.

Gorilla-man aimed a backhanded slap at Lizzie. She fell with a cry. In a fury Indy jumped on the man's back, knocking him to the floor again. The guy was a real animal. He bucked like a wild horse—and he had a kick like a mule.

Indy banged into a wall, hurting. He tottered to his feet, desperately trying to keep himself going.

Roberto was down too, with Dough-face and the other thug kicking him. Lizzie had fallen onto one of the beds, half-stunned. Things looked very bad for the good guys.

"Hey! Waddaya guys think you're doing?"

Silvio appeared in the apartment doorway. The stairs from the roof thundered with the sounds of many more approaching feet.

Dough-face turned to his henchmen. "Here comes trouble. Let's beat it!"

He jumped out the parlor window onto the fire escape. His pals followed. Neither Indy nor Roberto was in any shape to stop them.

A bunch of young Italian guys came running through the room and out the fire escape. Silvio knelt by his cousin. "Roberto!" he said. "You okay? We knew you was in here. Then we saw these other guys up on the roof. So we came to check things out."

He gazed at the three shaky people in the room, concern on his face. "Looks like we came along kinda late."

Roberto tried to sit up. A big bruise marred

his handsome cheek. "Thanks, Silvio. You were just in time." He glanced around, frowning. "But what about those guys who attacked us?"

"They're going nowhere," Silvio assured him. "The escape ladder is all fouled up, and the boys are on their trail."

From outside they heard the clatter of metal and a heavy impact. "Come on, you lily livers!" Dough-face shouted. "I jumped without the ladder, and it didn't hurt me!"

Indy ran to the window. "Those guys are getting away!" he yelled. "They're jumping from the second floor!"

Silvio joined him. "Those slobs are halfway down the block. Come on, guys!" he yelled to his friends. "After them! Don't let 'em get away!"

But Dough-face and his thugs disappeared around the corner. They were gone without a trace before any of Silvio's pals reached the sidewalk.

"Frankly," Indy admitted, "I'm glad they got away. They were killing us!"

Roberto sat on a tangled pile of bedding, holding his head. He seemed a little dazed from the beating he'd taken.

"Are you all right, Roberto?" Lizzie asked. Once again Indy could see that the concern in her eyes was more than just friendly. He sighed.

"So who were those mugs, Roberto?" Silvio wanted to know. "You seen them before? Maybe they set fire to this joint." He scowled and headed out the door. "But don't you worry. Me and the boys, we'll be looking for them."

"I'd just like to know where they came from," Lizzie said.

"We know of one person who'd send them," Indy said grimly. "Someone who hates Roberto. Who doesn't want him around anymore. Who'd be happy to steal anything Roberto might own." He turned to the young Italian man. "I think your boss has decided to play rough."

"Wilfred Frobisher," Lizzie whispered, her face pale.

Their conversation was interrupted by a wild cry.

"Roberto! What's the matter?" Lizzie asked, turning to him.

Roberto's face was as white as his torn shirt. His fingers plucked at his waistband.

"It's gone," he said, his voice almost numb with horror. "It must have happened during the fight. I never even felt it. . . ."

He began feverishly searching around the floor.

"What's gone?" Lizzie asked, completely puzzled. "What are you talking about?"

"The ruby cross," Indy said quickly, also starting to search the floor. "Roberto must have lost the cross during the fight."

Lizzie joined in looking around the torn-apart room for the cross. "It's big enough," she muttered, checking under a pile of bed-covers. "I mean, it really can't be lost."

"But it can be stolen," Roberto said in a tight voice.

"You mean those thugs *took* it from you during the fight?" Lizzie said.

Indy laughed shortly. "The way that fight was going, the bad guys could have taken a bed and we wouldn't have noticed." He continued to search the apartment, but it was obvious the cross wasn't there.

"I'm sorry you lost your family cross, Roberto," Lizzie said. From the look on her face, she was baffled. Why was the young man so shaken up?

"It's not just a family relic," Roberto said. His face was ash-white. "It's—it's like the soul of my family. The ruby cross—it has a curse on it."

"A curse?" Indy said.

"Whoever steals the cross—dies," Roberto said flatly.

"Well, that should teach the thief a lesson," Lizzie said, laughing lightly.

Roberto wasn't laughing. "There's more to the curse, though. It doesn't just settle on the thief. It also strikes the member of my family who let the cross be lost."

"What happens?" Lizzie asked, still laughing. "A seven-year itch?"

Roberto's eyes were somber and empty of hope. "Whoever loses the cross dies too. No matter what they do, they die."

Chapter 9

"You've got to be kidding!" Lizzie exclaimed. "Roberto, you don't really believe in this ancient curse sort of thing. Do you?"

Indy didn't know why Lizzie bothered to ask that question. The haunted look on Roberto Normanni's face was answer enough.

"Don't knock it," Indy said. "I've seen a lot of weird stuff in the last year. Enough so I don't laugh at ancient curses anymore." He turned to Roberto. "We'll get it back," he promised. "Whatever it takes, we'll get the cross back."

"If only we knew what Wilfred Frobisher will do with the cross," Lizzie said. "It's too bad we can't get into his mansion and find out what he's up to."

Indy frowned in thought. "But we do have a spy in that house." He smiled at Lizzie's puzzled look. "Minna Frobisher lives there, too, doesn't she?"

Laughing, Lizzie shook her head. "I surely don't know what's the matter with me today." Her worried glance at Roberto showed why she wasn't thinking clearly.

Lizzie reached into her handbag and brought out a little notebook. "I believe I even have Minna's telephone number with me."

"Good," Indy said. "Let's go find a public phone and give her a call." He hesitated. "And Lizzie—I don't think I'd tell whoever answers that I'm Lizzie Ravenall."

She nodded with a slightly embarrassed grin. "I'm not *that* scatterbrained," she said. She thought for a second, then grinned more widely. "Everyone at school says I can mimic one girl perfectly. That's the voice I'll use."

They found a public phone in a nearby hotel. Lizzie called the Frobisher mansion. "Hello, there," she said breezily into the receiver. Lizzie smiled at Roberto as she continued in a deeper-than-usual voice. "This is Susan Vandercross. Mama is having a bit of a do, and I'd like to invite dear Minna. May I talk to her? Oh. Oh, yes, I see. How sad." Her face fell and her voice slipped a little. "Well, perhaps when she's feeling better . . ."

She hung up the phone with a bang, looking furious. "That was a lie! They're saying that she has a touch of influenza and can't go out or see anyone." Lizzie looked glumly at her friends. "How can we get a message to her?"

Indy thought that over. Then a slow smile began to spread across his face. "Lizzie, do you have something for Roberto to write on? I think it's my turn."

Evening shadows were falling along Fifth Avenue. A blue-uniformed figure pedaled a bicycle to the gate of the Frobisher mansion and turned in. Then after taking a moment to polish the brass buttons on his uniform— and pull the uniform cap low over his eyes— Indy yanked on the bell knob.

The door opened to reveal a young chambermaid. Unruly red curls escaped from under her starched cap. Green eyes peered suspiciously out at Indy.

"Western Union!" Indy boldly announced. "Telegram for Miss Minna Frobisher."

The girl looked at him closely. "Sure, an' I've seen you before, with Miss Lizzie," she whispered. "I'll get the young mistress. You wait right here."

Indy stood in the front hall, a room as large as Aunt Mary's whole apartment. It was crammed with all sorts of expensive bric-a-brac, including at least two suits of armor. Indy didn't envy the servants who had to dust this place.

He shifted uncomfortably in his wool suit. It had taken a little time to find a willing messenger boy the right size. But the kid had given him not only the uniform but also an official Western Union message blank. The phony telegram in its envelope was pretty harmless—it told Minna that a nonexistent friend was coming to town. The real message he had to deliver was hidden in his pocket.

It was a note from Roberto, written in Italian. Lizzie was a little worried about the whole thing. "I know Minna takes Italian at

Barnard," she'd said. "But are you sure she'll understand what you're saying?"

Roberto had smiled. "She'll understand."

Well, Indy had gotten farther than Lizzie had. He could only hope . . .

Wilfred Frobisher suddenly appeared in the hallway. There was no chance for Indy to duck and hide. But Minna's brother hardly even glanced at him. "Is that the bid from Rockefeller?" he asked no one in particular. "I'll be in the study."

He stepped into a large room with pink marble pillars, not bothering to close the door. Frobisher threw himself into a chair. Then he rubbed his hands gleefully.

Indy shook his head. The man looked like a little boy with a secret. Frobisher picked up the telephone. "Hello, Central," he said to the operator on the other end. "Give me Murray Hill 3467."

A moment later he was chattering away on the phone. "It's incredible—a real medieval treasure," Frobisher said. "This ruby cross will open my way into real society. The big fellows—Rockefeller, Astor—they're all bidding for it. They'll have to accept me now."

"Excuse me." Minna Frobisher looked nervously around the hall. "My maid says there's a message for me."

"Yes, ma'am." Indy moved from where he'd been eavesdropping to hand the phony telegram to Minna.

"Here's a little something for you," Minna said, dropping a dime into Indy's hand.

"And here's something more important for you." Indy pulled the other note from his pocket.

Minna seemed to recognize the handwriting on the note. Her eyes got big as she took it.

"You—boy. What is this message you're delivering?" It was Marchbanks, the butler, appearing from a door at the back of the hall. The man stepped toward Indy, his hand outstretched. "Give it here—"

That's when he noticed Minna Frobisher standing in the hallway. "Ma'am, you know your brother doesn't want you to—"

The gloomy-looking butler suddenly stopped speaking and looked more carefully at Indy. "Wait a minute. I've seen you before."

If anything, Marchbanks' face became even

more gloomy. "You were here with that snippy Miss Ravenall." The butler turned to the door he'd appeared from. "William! Ronald! Come here quickly."

Two burly young footmen came out in response to Marchbanks' call. He pointed at Indy. "Remove this young man from the premises."

Heavy hands landed on Indy's arms. "Hey, guys, take it easy on the uniform. It's borrowed, you know."

Indy saw Minna Frobisher run up the stairs. At least she still had Roberto's message.

Although the two footmen were giving Indy the bum's rush, they weren't nasty about it. Getting tossed out of the house hurt Indy's dignity more than anything else. He got up, rubbed his behind where he'd landed, and jumped onto his bicycle.

Indy pedaled for about a block, until he reached the spot where Roberto and Lizzie waited anxiously for him.

"Well? What happened?" Lizzie asked.

"I was very lucky. Minna's maid answered the door and recognized me. She got Minna downstairs to get the telegram."

Roberto nodded. "She's a very under-standing one, that Nora." He glanced at Indy. "So—Minna got my note?"

Indy nodded. "I also saw Wilfred Frobisher. He seemed to think I was bringing a bid from Rockefeller."

"A bid?" Lizzie said, puzzled. "A bid for what?"

Indy glanced at Roberto. "For the cross, I think. Frobisher got on the telephone and was bragging about what a treasure it is. I know that Rockefeller collects stuff from the Middle Ages. Sometimes he hires my father to ad-vise him on it."

"So you not only got the message to Minna, you also managed to find out that Frobisher definitely has the cross." Lizzie looked very pleased. "Great work, Indy."

Roberto only groaned and sat down on the edge of the pavement.

Lizzie leaned anxiously over him, resting her hands on his shoulders. "Don't worry, Roberto. Now that we know he has your cross, we can—"

"We can do nothing," Roberto said heavily. "What are you going to suggest? Going to the police? Wilfred Frobisher is a rich man.

He *owns* more policemen than I have pennies. Do you think they're really going to arrest him on the word of a poor man?"

"But we know he's got the cross—" Lizzie began stubbornly.

"Indy *thinks* he has the cross. We have no proof." Roberto sighed. "No proof that anyone will listen to."

"So what are you going to do?" Indy wished he hadn't asked. He didn't like the grim look on Roberto's face.

"I will do the only thing a poor man can do when a rich man cheats him." Roberto still looked like a statue—but this time the title of the statue would be *Revenge*.

"I will find myself a knife," Roberto said. "And then I will cut Wilfred Frobisher's throat."

Chapter 10

"Roberto, no!" Lizzie turned horrified eyes on the handsome young man. "Promise me you won't do something that will get you hanged."

He smiled at her, although his eyes seemed a little feverish. "All right. If it makes you so upset, I'll promise. For now I'll only hurt Wilfred Frobisher with my mouth." He laughed. "I'll get all of his workers to join my union."

Roberto ran a hand across his forehead. "But first I think I'll rest a little. All of a sudden I don't feel so good."

Indy and Lizzie exchanged worried glances. Roberto didn't *look* very well, either. His eyes were glittering, as if he had a fever. And the skin on his face was so tight the bones seemed to show through.

Roberto wanted to take a streetcar home, but Lizzie wouldn't hear of it. She put Roberto into a cab, making sure he gave his latest address in Greenwich Village.

As the taxi took off, she looked worriedly at Indy. "What now?" Lizzie asked.

"I have to return this uniform and bike to the messenger boy who rented them to me," Indy said. "After that, I'd better get home."

"I'll give you a lift," Lizzie offered.

For a moment Indy felt flattered. Lizzie could have taken Roberto home. Instead she was traveling with him.

But as soon as they were in another cab, Indy found out why.

"I'm worried about Roberto," Lizzie admitted. Her hands were two tight little fists sitting on her knees. "He seems to take these family stories far too seriously."

"You mean, about the cross and how people die?" Indy asked.

She nodded.

"Well, you can't—"

"I think it has nothing to do with magic," Lizzie cut in. "It's like what happens in Africa or the West Indies. What do they call it? The power of suggestion. Where a medicine man convinces a person he's going to die of black magic. And"—her lips trembled—"because the person believes, he dies."

"Lizzie, you don't really think Roberto is going to—"

"I don't know what to think, Indy. I'm just so afraid for him." There were tears in Lizzie's eyes. "He's so brave, so strong—"

Awkwardly, Indy took Lizzie's hand and patted it. "Everything will be okay. You'll see. If Roberto needs help, I'll be there."

Lizzie tried to smile. "Oh, Indy, you've always been such a good friend to me!" She gave him an impulsive hug.

That's me, Indy thought. Just a good friend.

Her head on Indy's shoulder, Lizzie muttered something.

"What was that?" Indy said.

"I said, 'That stupid ruby cross.' And it *is* stupid, Indy. You saw the size of that gem. If the Normannis had sold it, they'd be rich. They could have afforded a fine farm, a good life for themselves. Maybe Roberto wouldn't be the last of his line. But no, they kept it in the family, hiding it all those years. Now he's so scared of it, it will be his death."

She choked back a sob, then said scornfully, "*Il Croce Ruggiero*—a fancy name to die for, it seems to me."

"What was that again?" Indy suddenly sat up very straight in the cab.

"*Il Croce Ruggiero*. That's what Roberto called the cross in Italian."

"So he did." Frowning, Indy tried to wiggle loose a memory from his brain. It was something his father had told him about. Something from all that research he'd been doing about the Normans.

"Lizzie," Indy said suddenly, "would you mind coming up to my aunt's apartment?"

"You want a witness to tell your folks that you haven't been up to any funny business?" Lizzie said with a sad smile. "I'll do my best, Indy. But I think your father was expecting *you* to keep an eye on *me*."

Aunt Mary was all prepared with another lecture. Then she saw they had a guest. Indy quickly introduced Lizzie. "Have you and Miss Ravenall eaten?" Aunt Mary asked.

"Uh, no," Indy said.

Immediately Aunt Mary began whipping a meal together. "Might have told me there'd be company," Indy heard her mutter as she set the table. "At least it's better than having you hare off on your own."

She gave Indy a look. "I hope you spent some time at the museum today. You were to look at the art collection, remember?"

"That's just what we did," Lizzie said brightly.

Indy gave her a grateful smile. "Yeah—right." He glanced nervously around the apartment. "By the way, where's Dad?"

"Your father had a lecture to give. He was called at the last minute to talk about Norman art of the Dark Ages. This fellow was setting it up on very short notice. Apparently a group of wealthy collectors wanted to know a lot about the subject in a hurry."

Indy stopped filling the water glasses and stared at his aunt. "This fellow who called," he said after a second. "His name wasn't Frobisher, was it?"

Aunt Mary looked surprised. "Why, so it was," she said. "Fancy your knowing that."

As Indy and Lizzie sat down to supper, Indy said, "I guess Dad will be home late."

"That's right," Aunt Mary said.

"Lizzie and I had a question for Dad about the Normans. But maybe we can find the answer ourselves in the books he's reading."

His aunt shook her head. "You like to live dangerously, don't you, young man? You know the one thing your father won't tolerate is someone disturbing his desk."

"We'll be careful," Indy promised.

After supper, Indy and Lizzie moved into the parlor. Professor Jones's desk was piled high with books. He must have plundered several libraries to get his dope about the Normans. Stuck here and there in the pile were sheets of notes.

"What do we need to find out about the Normans?" Lizzie whispered. "William the Conqueror, 1066. That's when they conquered England. Everybody learns that in history class."

"There's a lot more about the Normans that everybody doesn't know." Indy tapped one set of notes. "They were Vikings—sea raiders—who took over a piece of French coast. A hundred and fifty years later they were a major power that conquered England. Thirty years after that, Norman knights joined the First Crusade to save the Holy Land from the Saracens. They ended up carving out their own kingdom at Antioch."

He dug deeper into the pile. "Here it is—Italy. Twenty years before William sailed to England, there were Norman knights in southern Italy. Local nobles hired the knights to do their fighting for them." Indy began paging through the books on the desk. One of them had to be in English, not some ancient tongue.

"Here's the name I was trying to remember." He closed a thick book. "A Norman knight named Robert de Hauteville became a duke in southern Italy. He sent his brother Roger over to conquer the island of Sicily in 1061. In those days Sicily was held by the Saracens. Roger's war was like a dress rehearsal for the Crusades. For thirty years the Normans fought, and finally Sicily was theirs."

Lizzie frowned. "So? How does that apply to the problems we're facing right now"—her voice trembled a little—"with Roberto?"

"Dad's been tracking down a legend." Indy was skimming his father's notes. "Hey, here it is."

He read for a second, then explained. "Some of the old writers mention a sword carried by Roger de Hauteville. It was supposed to be magic, to help him attack the Saracens. The hilt of the sword had a gem of great power. Tales tell of the sword helping Normans to win victories even though they were heavily outnumbered. Roger seemed to believe in it. To protect the sword and keep it in his family, he put a great curse on it. Whoever stole the sword would die. And whichever member of his family let the sword be lost would die as well."

Indy looked up from the notes. "Sounds familiar, doesn't it?"

Frowning, Lizzie asked, "What happened to this sword, anyway?"

Indy went back to reading. "It says here that Roger gave the sword to his son, who became the first king of Sicily and southern

Italy. Then it seems to disappear. Soon after, the Norman kingdom disappeared, too."

Lizzie shook her head. "Okay, we've got a sword with a curse on it. I guess that shows how people thought in those days. But Roberto's family is Italian, not Norman—"

"Think about Roberto's last name," Indy interrupted. "I don't know much Italian, but I can translate that. Normanni means 'of the Normans.' I can also translate *Il Croce Ruggiero*."

He looked carefully at Lizzie. "It comes out to 'The Cross of Roger.'"

Lizzie was shaken by Indy's words. But she was also stubborn. "That's a cross," she pointed out. "You were talking about a sword."

"When you've got to hide something for eight hundred and fifty years, a lot of changes can be made." Indy went back to the notes. "There's a lot more here about the sword and its hilt. According to the old historians, you could call on Roger's spirit for help. They even give the proper words and phrases in Latin. That's the language everyone used back then for formal stuff."

"I don't want to hear any more of these crazy legends," Lizzie said angrily. "Thanks for the history lesson, Indiana Jones!"

"Henry? Giving a history lesson? Will wonders never cease!" Aunt Mary came into the room, surprised but happy. "I'm glad to see you applying yourself to some studies, young man."

Then she gave Indy a stern look. "What I haven't seen, though, is your composition on the Metropolitan Museum."

"I'll get on it right away," Indy promised. "Right after Lizzie leaves."

"And speaking of *that*, I should be going," Lizzie said, rising to her feet. "We have an early curfew at Barnard, and I don't want to be getting in trouble."

Indy walked her downstairs, where they waited for a taxi. "I still think all the stuff you said is crazy," Lizzie said. "But I *am* worried about Roberto. I'm going to be stuck in the dean's office tomorrow discussing my course of study. So I'm depending on you, Indy."

She turned pleading eyes on him. "Watch over Roberto for me, will you?"

"I'll do my best," Indy promised. He waved good-bye as she got into a taxi. Then he went upstairs to write about his visit to the museum. All he could remember was the medieval armor and swords.

The next morning Indy was up early, heading down to Greenwich Village. He doled out a precious nickel to ride the subway— time was short. Even so, he barely reached the address where Roberto was staying before the young Italian came out.

This was not the strong, fresh Roberto who had carried blocks of stone on his shoulders. Instead, this Roberto moved like an old man. His skin was yellowish and seemed even more tightly drawn over his cheekbones. He didn't look well at all. Lizzie had been right to be worried.

Indy trailed along behind Roberto, keeping his presence a secret. He suspected Roberto wouldn't want to be caught looking like this. It broke his heart to see Roberto pulling himself up the stair rail to the El station at Ninth Street and Sixth Avenue.

Lagging behind meant that Indy had to

dash quickly to pay his fare. A train was coming in. He hopped aboard at the last moment, just before the doors closed. Another late passenger fought the closing doors in the next car up.

From the doorway of his own car Indy caught a glimpse of the latecomer's face—heavy, flabby, pale. A chill ran down his spine. He recognized that guy. It was Dough-face—the man who'd led the attack on them in Roberto's apartment.

What was that thug doing here on the train?

Chapter 11

Indy was afraid he knew the answer to that question. Plowing through the rush-hour crowd, he headed into the next car, where Dough-face was.

Indy didn't have to search far to find the thug. The crowd had almost magically parted to make an open space around the grim-looking man.

Dough-face didn't notice Indy. His attention was on Roberto Normanni. Roberto slumped against the door on the far end of the car, his eyes closed. He didn't even see the thug's murderous advance.

The crowd closed behind Dough-face as he moved forward. Indy fought to force a path

through the riders. They paid little attention to him—and nobody noticed the action
at the far end of the car.

Dough-face's broad back hid most of the
scene as he shoved Roberto out the door.
Now they were alone on the small open-air
platform between cars. Frantically Indy in-
creased his pace. He cannoned out the door
just as Dough-face was trying to bundle a
surprised Roberto over the left-hand railing.

Indy gulped, looking down at the gap between the two sets of tracks. It would be a
two-story fall to the hard cobblestone street
below.

The noise of the train drowned out
Roberto's croaking cry for help. Indy knew
it was up to him. He joined his hands together in a double fist and hammered down
on Dough-face's shoulder.

The thug only staggered a little. At least
that gave Roberto a chance to pull himself
away from the railing. But Dough-face shot
out a heavy hand to grab the front of
Roberto's shirt. The roughneck's other fist
smashed backhanded at Indy.

It caught Indy in the chest with such force,
he went flying toward the railing on the other

side of the platform. Indy teetered there for a moment, staring in terror at the storefronts below. A little more push and he'd have been making that long fall himself.

Roberto had one hand on the door handle to the next car. But Dough-face's big fist was twisted in the collar of Roberto's shirt. He hauled Roberto back, shoving him to the edge of the platform. Roberto fell.

The thug stood triumphantly over him. "The other boys felt too sick to take care of you, Normanni. But I'm never too sick to croak a guy."

Indy shoved off from the railing behind Dough-face. His arms just didn't have enough muscle to deal with this guy. He'd have to use his legs. Indy's foot shot out to catch Dough-face just behind his right knee. The thug's knee unlocked, throwing him off balance.

At the same moment, still lying on the platform, Roberto flung both legs at Dough-face's gut.

They couldn't have planned a move like that. Roberto's feet flung the tottering killer up and back. He shot back to the rail, eyes wide, arms windmilling frantically. Indy ducked the flailing arms as the killer went over.

Dough-face had time for one desperate wail before he hit the street.

Indy grabbed Roberto. "We've got to get out of here. Come on!"

They were the first ones off the train when it reached the next station.

Indy blew his remaining pocket money on a cab to take Roberto up to the Hotel Frobisher. "Are you sure you want to go to work?" he asked Roberto with a nervous glance. Roberto looked even worse than he had when he got on the train. He was bent over on his seat, his skin like parchment.

But his eyes glittered as he looked over at Indy. "I'm not going to work. I'm going to get fired."

Indy had to help Roberto down out of the cab when they reached the construction site. But the Italian threw Indy's arm aside as he stepped up to the crowd of workers waiting at the gates.

"*Santa Maria,* Roberto," one of the masons said, staring. "What happened to you?"

"Wilfred Frobisher tried to have me killed," Roberto said in a loud voice. "I was nearly thrown off the El." Roberto's chiseled nose stood out like a beak. The only touch of color on his drawn face was the pink scar over his eyebrow.

The group of men buzzed with anger. "You don't look so good," another workman said.

"This is the way we'll all look if we let rich vampires like Frobisher suck us dry!" Roberto's voice was loud and angry. "There's only one way to protect ourselves from being picked off one by one." Now his voice began to fail.

"The union!" he croaked. "Only with a union can we—"

Roberto's lips moved for a couple of seconds, but no words came out. Swaying, he stared down at himself as if he'd suddenly received an awful surprise. He tried to speak again. Then he collapsed.

"What do you mean, he's dying and you have no idea why?" Lizzie Ravenall's flushed face was only inches from the grave face of the doctor. Her bonnet was on at a strange angle. She had crammed it on her head and rushed to the hospital as soon as Indy had called her.

"Is he sick? Maybe he got injured in the fight." Her blue eyes darkened. "Or maybe he's been poisoned. He has enemies, you know, powerful enemies—"

"So you've told me, Miss Ravenall," the doctor interrupted. "Several times. Be that as it may, I can only report the facts. Mr. Normanni seems to be a strong young man. Yet his life appears to be—" The doctor hesitated, shrugging his shoulders. "It's just leaking away. There is nothing physically wrong with him. But in the last fifteen minutes he's slipped into a coma."

"Well, what are you going to do about it?" Lizzie asked frantically.

The doctor looked down at the tiled hospital floor. "I'm sorry, young lady. There's nothing we *can* do." He glanced over at her. "Besides pray." He walked off down the corridor.

Lizzie peeked into the hospital room. She'd ordered the best care for Roberto, taken on the best doctors. Money was no object. But Roberto just lay on the bed, still and pale.

She turned back to Indy. "This is crazy. *Crazy!* He's so big and strong—you saw what he did with those stone blocks. How can he be dying? *How?*"

"It's the cross," Indy said grimly. *"Il Croce Ruggiero.* The curse—"

"Stop trying to distract me with that mumbo jumbo." Lizzie glared at him angrily. "Do you really believe he's dying because someone stole his magic cross?"

"Lizzie, since the last time I saw you in Washington, I've bumped into a magic crown, two magic rings, and magic fire. If I've learned one thing, it's not to knock what I don't understand."

Indy grabbed her hand. "At least there's something we can *do*—instead of just waiting for the end. Come on. Back to the Frobishers'!"

Lizzie let herself be bundled into a cab. But she began to have doubts during the ride uptown. "This is a wild-goose chase," she complained.

"No, it's not," said Indy. "Roberto's note to Minna Frobisher asked her to find out where the cross is. If she finds out, she's supposed to listen for our signal and get a message to us."

"*If* she finds out. *If* she can get us a message. I should have stayed at the hospital. . . ."

They got out of the cab about a block away from the Frobisher mansion. The pink stone building glittered in the sunlight. "Come on, Minna," Lizzie whispered as they came closer.

Walking along the wall, Indy began whistling. He thought they'd chosen a good tune for the signal—"She's Only a Bird in a Gilded Cage." He'd reached the second chorus when an upstairs window opened. A hand appeared between the drapes, tossing something out. At first it looked like a handkerchief, but it hit the pavement with a solid *clink*.

Lizzie pounced on the little white package. "There's a note in here, wrapped up in the hankie." She nearly tore it open.

"Right—weighted down with silver dollars." Indy moved to corral the big silver coins before they rolled away. They'd pay for a whole lot of cabs. "What does Minna say?"

"Wilfred is keeping the cross in a bank vault," Lizzie told him, her shoulders slumping in defeat. Then her head came up.

"But he's going to auction it off to the highest bidder at a big dinner at Delmonico's this evening at eight!"

"Delmonico's—that's the swankiest restaurant in New York!" Indy exclaimed.

"The dinner auction is being held in a private dining room—by invitation only. Wilfred has asked the richest men in Society to come. They all collect art, and they're apparently fascinated with this cross."

"I guess Wilfred figures that once they come to his party, they'll have to invite him back," Indy said. "He was bragging about that when I overheard him on the phone." He shook his head. "The problem is, this is a private party, and the only guests will be rich old men." Glancing at Lizzie and then down at himself, he laughed. "I think they'll notice if we try to stroll in there."

But by the time the clock crept toward eight that evening, Indy and Lizzie were inside Delmonico's.

"I don't think this is such a good idea," Indy muttered nervously. He tugged at the neckerchief on his busboy's uniform. The stupid thing seemed to be choking him. "You told the manager that we were professionals who'd been serving tables for years. I'm not even sure where all the silverware goes!"

"All you have to do is pick up empty plates," Lizzie whispered back. "At least you don't have to parade around in this getup." She gestured toward the trim little waitress outfit she wore. "This thing is positively immodest! The skirt is so short it nearly shows my knees. And these little slippers—you can see my ankles!"

Indy glanced down and his face went red. "You sure can," he choked out. "You have very pretty ankles, Lizzie."

Her face went a little pink. "That's sweet of you to say, Indy. But now we've got to find where that auction is going to be."

They wandered around the kitchens of the restaurant—big, cavernous rooms with walls of rough concrete. Ugly gray pillars held up the ceiling, and everywhere underneath, plain wooden tables held a variety of food. Indy saw everything from plucked chickens to a half-finished pastry shell decorated with someone's family crest.

"We're ready to start serving the Frobisher party," a man by the door said.

All but invisible in their uniforms, Lizzie

and Indy grabbed trays and trailed behind the other servers. They marched along a grim-looking unpainted hallway until the head waiter reached a big oak door.

When he threw it open, it was like stepping into another world. The private dining room had a big, thick Oriental rug in glowing reds and blues. The white linen tablecloth was dazzling in the light of the huge crystal chandelier that hung from the ceiling. Light sparkled off the crystal glasses and polished silverware on the main table. It reflected in a more muted way off the richly polished walnut paneling and rose silk wall-covering.

Everyone sitting in the room wore black tail coats, starched white shirts, and carefully knotted bow ties. The beautiful evening clothes said Money with a capital *M*. The only jarring note was the faces of the guests. They were all old and wrinkled. Frown lines cut in around the mouths. Whatever hair the men had left was white.

There was only one youngish person at the table: Wilfred Frobisher. Indy had to hold back a gasp when he saw him. Frobisher looked very different from the man who'd threatened Lizzie and boasted over the phone.

His face was even redder than the last time Indy had seen him, but it didn't seem healthy. Sweat beaded on Frobisher's forehead and cheeks. The flesh on his face hung in flabby pink jowls. His piggy little eyes glittered as if he had a fever.

"Frobisher, old man," said a rich codger with white chin whiskers. "You don't look too well. Ought to try some of the new health cereals my company is coming out with. We're making these new wheat flakes—"

"Thank you, Amory," Wilfred Frobisher said. "It's just the excitement. After all, it's not often one gets to display a treasure like this—"

He whipped open a rosewood case at his elbow, displaying *Il Croce Ruggiero*. "Apparently it was brought over here by some Italian yokel who didn't realize its value. I recognized it for what it was, very early Norman work, and just—"

Indy stepped forward, shouting in a loud voice, "And you just stole it. We saw your thugs do the job!"

Chapter 12

Indy couldn't believe the uproar he caused. Probably all the captains of industry at the table had been called thieves at some point in their careers. But they were shocked to hear the accusation in Delmonico's.

The heavy hands of waiters and busboys landed on Indy's shoulders. These guys had been flattering the people at the table for years. Their tips depended on it. Indy was marched to the door.

Lizzie stepped forward. "Every word my friend says is true! Wilfred Frobisher sent thugs to attack Roberto Normanni because he's trying to organize a union—"

Those words brought a growl of protest

from the assembled wealthy men. They didn't like unions.

"And they stole Roberto's family treasure! He's just a big thief and liar . . . Hey! Get your hands off me!"

In a moment Lizzie had been surrounded as well and was being dragged away.

"Sir," the headwaiter said to a purple-faced Wilfred Frobisher, "should we get the police to deal with these mad people?"

"Serve them right to be clapped into jail," said Mr. Wheat-flakes.

Indy thought fast. An idea popped into his head. "Sure, Frobisher," he yelled from the door. "Auction off the ruby cross. Let somebody else discover the treasure inside."

"What treasure?" Greed shone in every line of Frobisher's flabby face.

"If you'd talked to Roberto, you'd have known that the cross comes apart. Just press the little stud hidden on one of the arms and pull."

"There *is* a little stud," Frobisher exclaimed as he examined the cross carefully. "Maybe this is even more valuable than I thought."

He pulled the cross apart. Now one thick arm was in his left hand, while his right held a T-shaped piece of metal. Yes, Indy thought, those thin gold arms, the thicker body. He should have recognized it sooner. He'd seen enough of them at the museum of art. *Il Croce Ruggiero* wasn't a cross. It was the hilt of a sword *disguised* as a cross.

Indy began chanting in Latin. *"Veni, Rogere, veni!"* He hoped he remembered all the words he'd seen written in his father's notes.

"What the—?" Wilfred Frobisher burst out, staring at the hilt in his hand. The ruby in the center of the cross was glowing with a light of its own. It flashed brilliantly three times, almost blinding the people in the room.

At first Indy thought his dazzled eyes were tricking him. The hilt wasn't empty anymore. Rising mistily from the metal T in Frobisher's right hand was a four-foot blade.

Frobisher stared at the ghostly sword, surprise in his piggy eyes. The guests at the table stared beyond him. Moans of terror clogged their throats.

The air in the room seemed suddenly to be twenty degrees colder.

Now the hands holding Indy disappeared as the waiters shrank back in fear. When they moved away, Indy finally saw what was frightening everyone.

Standing behind Wilfred Frobisher was a tall figure. It was dressed in a shirt made of chain mail—ancient armor from the Dark Ages. And the reason for everyone's fear was obvious. They could see through the figure to the silken wallcovering beyond it!

Even as they watched, the phantom became more solid. They couldn't see much of its face—it wore a tall conical helmet with a bar of iron that descended to protect the nose. But they could see the frown on the lips, the fury in the brilliant blue eyes. The skin of the figure—its face and hands—was dead-white, like living stone. And the chill in the room deepened as it stepped forward.

"Who—*what* is that?" Lizzie whispered, coming to stand beside Indy.

"That's Roger de Hauteville, Count of Sicily, father of the first Norman king—Ruggiero. And I think he wants his sword."

Count Roger now stood beside Wilfred

Frobisher's seat. A ghostly hand came down on a well-padded shoulder.

Frobisher jumped as if he'd been touched by an icicle. He turned from the ghostly sword he'd been staring at—and looked up into Roger de Hauteville's cold blue eyes.

The rich young man's jowly jaw dropped, and a strangled noise came out of his mouth. He looked as if he wanted to leap up from his seat and run out of the room. But he didn't dare try to shrug that icy white hand off his shoulder.

The ghostly blade shimmered now as the hilt shook in Frobisher's trembling hand. He was alone at the head of the table. All the rich bidders huddled at the other end, not sure what to do—and not willing to come too close.

So there was no one to stand in the way as Count Roger plucked the sword from Frobisher's quivering grasp. The phantom seemed all business as it tested the heft of the blade. Then with its left hand the spirit seized Frobisher by the chin, forcing his head back, exposing his throat. The edge of the ghost sword came down to slice—

"No!" shouted Indy. Roger de Hauteville's

cold blue eyes came up to pin him in a stare.

"Ne iugula!" Indy cried in Latin. "Don't kill him!" For once he was glad for his father and Aunt Mary. They'd insisted he study this dead language. Now it was the only chance to keep Wilfred Frobisher alive.

"This thief's blood should not stain your sword," Indy went on in Latin. "Let me return it to the one who truly owns the cross."

For a long moment the eyes of a man who had lived 850 years ago bored into Indy. Then, after that measuring gaze, Roger de Hauteville nodded. He tossed the sword on the table and let go of Wilfred Frobisher.

Indy stared at the whimpering bulk in front of him. Frobisher was gasping like a beached fish, but the normal red color was coming back to his face. Or rather, to most of his face. The spot where Roger de Hauteville's icy palm had rested—the chin—remained bloodless.

And the prints of the ghost's fingers and thumb showed up, dead-white, on Wilfred Frobisher's cheeks and jowls.

Indy moved to pick up the hilt. It was freezing cold to the touch, but the ruby in the center was losing its glow. Wrapping a thick napkin around the cold metal, he held the hilt up. The sword blade had faded away. With no trouble Indy was able to slip the removable arm into place, turning the sword hilt back into a cross.

He glanced up to look for Count Roger of Sicily. But the phantom had disappeared.

"We'll be leaving with this now," he announced to everyone in the room. "I've promised to return the ruby cross to its rightful owner."

The titans of industry stayed huddled at their end of the table. Some stared at the cross. Others stared at the strange white prints on Wilfred Frobisher's face.

But no one bothered Indy and Lizzie as they left the room.

They ran out onto Fifth Avenue and hailed a cab. Indy climbed aboard, holding the cross still wrapped in the napkin. Lizzie gave the address of the hospital, crying, "Don't hold the horses! It's a matter of life and death!"

The cabbie nodded and moved the cab as fast as he could. Indy and Lizzie sat in silence. At last Indy turned to her and asked, "So what do you think of mumbo jumbo now?"

"I'll tell you later," Lizzie whispered. "If we save Roberto's life."

Together they rushed down the hospital corridor. Roberto's aunt and uncle, his cousin Silvio, and several friends stood around the door of his room. So did the long-faced doctor whom Lizzie had hired, along with a nurse and a man in a black robe—a priest!

"Are we—" Lizzie choked.

From inside the room they heard the sound of weeping. They looked through the doorway to find Minna Frobisher holding Roberto's hand and crying.

"Minna!" Lizzie burst out. "What are you doing here?"

"One of the servants at home knew what had happened to Roberto. My maid heard." Minna lifted a tear-stained face. "She told me, and I—I ran away. Cut up a sheet to make a rope and climbed down from my bedroom window."

She turned back to the still form on the bed. "Oh, Roberto, Roberto! We had to keep it secret, but . . . but we were in love."

"In love?" Lizzie looked as if she'd been hit in the head with a hammer.

"We've known each other for more than a

year. I went to hear him talk about the union
. . . so brave, so handsome." She began to
cry again. "How could I not fall in love with
him? And then, miracle of miracles, I found
out he felt the same way about me."

"In love . . ." Lizzie repeated dully.

Indy approached the bed, afraid he was
too late. Roberto looked more dead than
alive. Indy unwrapped the ruby cross and
placed it on Roberto's chest. For a second
the young man lay there, terrifyingly still.

Then, amazingly, Roberto's eyes fluttered
open. "M-Minna?" he breathed. Feeling the
weight on his chest, he glanced down. "My
cross?"

He looked up, dumbstruck, at Indy and
Lizzie standing nearby. "You—you—but how
could you—? What—?"

Minna was crying again, but now they
were tears of joy. She and Roberto em-
braced.

Indy caught Lizzie's elbow. "Maybe we
should get out of here and leave them alone,"
he said.

They stepped out of the room and into the
rejoicing knot of people in the corridor. There
were tears and whoops of joy and thankful

prayers. Indy and Lizzie got away as quickly as they could.

Lizzie was quiet as they left the hospital. Indy felt a little sorry for her. She'd fought so hard for Roberto, only to learn . . .

"I'm sorry," he finally said. "I guess things didn't work out as you hoped."

Lizzie gave him a funny little smile. "Sometimes life is like that." Indy took her hand and gave it a squeeze.

Lizzie walked along silently for a while. Then she suddenly laughed. "At least Roberto won't have to worry about where to keep his ruby cross anymore," she said wryly. "Rich folks like the Frobishers always know where to hide their loot."

Indy laughed too. This sounded more like the Lizzie he knew.

"And I've still got the vote to fight for— and some good friends," she said. "Promise me one thing, Indy."

"Anything," he said.

"Wherever you go, whatever mumbo jumbo you get involved in—remember me."

"That's a promise," he said. "By the way, do you know anything about famous paintings?"

"A little," Lizzie said. "Why?"

"I still have to finish up that report on the Metropolitan Museum of Art," Indy explained.

Lizzie looked puzzled.

"Well, you're the one who told Aunt Mary I saw the pictures. You don't want to make a liar out of me, do you?"

Lizzie began laughing. "Heaven forbid, Indiana Jones," she said. "Heaven forbid!"

HISTORICAL NOTE

The Normans—who get their name from the French word for "Northman"—were very real. They started out as Vikings, swooping down from what is now Scandinavia to raid the French coast. Some decided to stay. By the year 1066 they were rewriting the history of the world.

Norman knights led by Duke William sailed across the English channel and conquered England. Wandering Norman knights built themselves another kingdom in Italy. Their skill at war allowed small Norman armies to defeat much larger enemy forces. A handful of blue-eyed Norman adventurers wound up ruling half of Italy—and the island of Sicily. Their kingdom faded away by the year 1200. But Norman blood still runs in Italian families. Sometimes travelers find Sicilians with blue eyes—like the character in this story, Roberto Normanni.

Several medieval historians wrote about the Norman kingdom, including the men discussed by Professor Jones and Dean Sayers in her office. Count Roger of Sicily is a historical conqueror. But the legend of his sword (and *Il Croce Ruggiero*) is found only in this book.

Roberto Normanni may not be real, but the contribution of immigrant Italians like him can still be seen. Immigrants were an important part of the New York work force in the early 1900s. They helped build the new subways and worked to erect many of the new buildings—skyscrapers—which were changing the Manhattan skyline. It was a time of dangerous labor conditions and much struggle for working people. One of the ways they joined together for protection was in labor unions. To work as a union organizer was a risky job.

Another risky job was to fight for the vote for women. An unsuccessful campaign for female suffrage had been waged for decades, but after 1910 the battle heated up. Militant suffragettes began marching—even picketing the President. The fight got hotter after the events of this story. Between 1917 and 1919 more than five hundred women were arrested for protesting over the vote. Not till 1920 did the suffragettes finally win their war. That year the Nineteenth Amendment to the U.S. Constitution gave the vote to American women.

New York, by 1900, was the leading city of the U.S.A. A great building boom was on to make it the tallest. It was a very different city from the one we know today. The first skyscraper (the Flatiron Building, built in 1902) had a modest 21 stories. By the time Indy arrived in New York for this story, the Woolworth Building rose 60 floors—792 feet—the highest building in the world for nearly twenty years. Most of the New York places in this book actually exist—but not the Frobisher mansion and the Hotel Frobisher.

Cars were just beginning to appear in numbers on New York City streets. At first they were mainly taxicabs and limousines. There was still a lot of horse-drawn traffic, especially in quieter neighborhoods.

The elevated trains had switched over from steam locomotives to electrical power. But in the years since this adventure, most of the Els have disappeared. Tracks that ran up Sixth and Ninth avenues have been taken down.

Delmonico's was a real restaurant, but the original one doesn't exist anymore. However, it lives on in menus everywhere, thanks to a dish called the Delmonico steak.

TO FIND OUT MORE, CHECK OUT . . .

The Good Old Days—They Were Terrible! by Otto L. Bettmann. Published by Random House, 1974. Fascinating photographs and old drawings reveal the hardships faced by Americans (especially New Yorkers) from the end of the Civil War through the early 1900s. The text is written for adults, but the pictures need little explaining. The dangerous working conditions that led people like Roberto Normanni to organize for labor unions, the awful housing of most city dwellers, and the horrors endured by immigrants crossing the ocean in steerage are just a few of the gripping subjects included. You won't be able to put this book down.

This Fabulous Century, Volume II, 1910–1920, by the editors of Time-Life Books. Published by Time-Life Books, 1969. A big, beautifully illustrated book about life in the United States between 1910 and 1920. Lively reading for all ages. Covers many topics of interest to Indy, such as early automobiles and New York theater, and much, much more. Don't miss the firsthand account of one woman's experience in a New York City suffrage parade, only a year after Lizzie's march up Broadway. Photographs, drawings; some in color.

The Story of the Nineteenth Amendment by R. Conrad Stein. Published by Children's Press, 1982. A history of the movement to grant women the right to vote in the United States. Shows just how hard it was for suffragettes like

Lizzie to stand up against their many male *and* female opponents. Drawings.

Ellis Island by William Jay Jacobs. Published by Charles Scribner's Sons, 1990. Moving photographs and an interesting, easy text portray the experience of immigrants entering the United States in the early 1900s. Really gives you a feel for how hopeful—and frightened—people like Roberto Normanni's family were when they arrived in America.

Gateway to America: New York City (The Dream of America series) by Erik V. Krustrup. Published by Creative Education, Inc., 1982. What was New York City like in the early part of this century? And how did it get that way? This history of the city takes a good hard look at immigrant life. Also touched on are the millionaire's New York and the formation of labor unions. Photographs, drawings.

The Normans (Peoples of the Past books) by Patrick Rooke. Published by Macdonald Educational, 1977. The story of the Normans from their first settling in France through their conquest of England and southern Italy to their final mysterious disappearance. Lively color drawings, photographs, and maps illustrate all aspects of Norman culture. The short biographies of famous Normans include an account of Roger de Hauteville (whose ghost helps Indy rescue Roberto Normanni's stolen cross).